SEEK TO LOVE

Seeking in Romance Book 4

KEKE RENÉE

304 Publishing Company

By Keke Renée:

Wet Heat

His Peace, Her Pleasure

Baby, It's Cold Outside

Love Don't Live Here Anymore, Book 1, 2

Every Time We Touch (A Wet Heat Novelette)

One Night Only-A Novelette - Love by Design Book 1

Cassian and Savannah - Love by Design Book 2

Deidra's Love - Love by Design Book 3

Protecting Bria (Special Forces Operation Alpha)

Haven

Taste

Sensual

Seek To Please

Seek To Bare

Seek To Touch

Upcoming 2022 releases

Seek To Trust

Seek To Earn

INTRODUCTION

Are you signed up for my newsletter?

Join today and find out all the latest in new releases, contests, giveaways, sneak peeks and more.

https://BookHip.com/ZXCKSSF

DISCLAIMER

THIS WORK OF FICTION contains strong language and explicit sexual content and is only intended for mature readers. This story may contain unconventional situations, language, and sexual encounters that may offend some readers. I would recommend selecting another book. This book is for mature readers (18+).

SYNOPSIS

Chelsey

Sometimes in relationships things run their course, but I thought we would never be that couple. I wanted my Happily ever after to continue, but love isn't about the good times, and learning myself everyday in this relationship has brought out a different side of me.

Xavier

She's the one that approached me. I tried to leave her alone, but now we're too deep into things to let anyone come between us. I refuse to let her go and will work to stop anyone, even her own thoughts from causing us to end.

Note: These characters first appeared in (Wet Heat). Seeking in Romance novelette series is dealing with Adult language, explicit content.

XAVIER

I snatched the door open, stomped into my office, and dropped my bag down on the floor. Exhausted from staying up late with Chelsey to make up for our busy schedules. She was at some girls' night, out having drinks and dinner. While I decided to come in and get caught up on some paperwork for my business. I was working for myself now, and that demanded a lot more of my time. The last time we spoke was at breakfast; she told me her day was booked up. I knew with me opening a second gym and possibly a third, depending on the negotiations, it would have a big impact on us spending time together. Chelsey was overseeing multiple banks now under her family's business. Her father still could be an asshole and barely spoke unless I initiated the conversation. Plus, having her new nephew around made me excited to want to try for our own kids. Jordan and Emma were constantly letting him stay over unless her parents requested for him during the week. It was around eight at night, and my stomach growled from the lack of food. I'd packed a few items for the road to snack on while I went through the updated permits and leasing information. Ever since we became friends with Mason and his friends at Club Seek, my world had changed for the better, and my clientele had increased. No longer did I have to advertise to get people to come into my business. I still had a high ratio of single women or new moms who wanted to lose weight; everything came word of mouth. A knock at the door caught my attention, and I glanced up to see Chelsey push it open, stroll inside, and come around my desk. She leaned over with her hand on the top of my shoulder.

"When did you—"

She placed her middle finger on top of my lips to cut me off.

"No questions," she replied, removing the pen and paper out of my hand. She dropped to her knees, unzipped my pants, and pulled out her favorite toy.

"You really missed me, huh?" She licked her full lips, opened her mouth, gripped the base of my dick, and kissed the tip. I reached to grasp the back of her head, and she smacked my hand away. No longer the shy, soft-spoken girl I knew growing up. Peanut transformed before my eyes and became a woman who knew what she wanted.

"Shit... Chelsey."

I watched as her eyes stared back up at me, and I almost lost control. My blood pressure rose as she took control of my body, but the pressure of my seed rose to the tip. I gritted my teeth as my toes cracked, and I felt her hands roam across my thighs.

"Take all of it down your throat," I demanded, as her head bobbed up and down. I gazed at how she took the last remnants of my cum and wiped her mouth with the back of her hand. Chelsey stared into my eyes as she moved from her knees to sitting on the edge of desk, with her legs spread and her dress raised over her thighs.

"Come and eat." She threw her head back, anticipating my lips upon her sweet nectar.

I stood, stroking myself, and lined up to her entrance as her breath caught in her throat with my initial push. Our skin warmed as I picked up the pace, trailing kisses along her chest and taking both breasts in my hand. She palmed the back of my head, as I latched onto her erect nipples, flicking my tongue, groping, and pressing them together to feel the cozy full breasts I loved to call home. I nudged my head up, shoving my tongue in her mouth, and clasped a hand around her throat, rocking back and forth in her sex. The sounds of her cries and moans reverberated in my ears, letting me know the dominance I put forth paid off. Finally moving my hands to her plump ass, I squeezed tightly, speeding up my pumps.

. "Shit," I grunted, feeling her pussy holding me hostage, and gripped the side of the desk. I whispered in her ear how good she felt to me. "You've ruined me for anyone else."

Her eyes lustfully drew open, and her upper lip curved up. "You've damaged me from anyone else."

That saying sparked something in me, and I growled, thrusted faster, and moved a hand to her clit to get her to the end of the line. Her screams in my ear let me know I was right behind her.

"Xavier, I'm coming."

"Fuck! Right behind you, Peanut." I picked her up off the desk, and slipped out. She dropped to her knees and pulled my dick in her mouth, sucking out the last remnants of my seed.

"What are you doing here?"

I helped her stand, watching her put her clothes back on. I sipped up my pants and fixed the papers on my desk.

"Dinner with the girls was fun, but I missed you."

"Yeah."

She sat in the chair in my office.

"I feel like we've been working so much, we don't have time for each other."

"Same."

"So, what do we do about this?"

I sighed, not feeling up to an argument.

"I'm not sure."

Her brow cocked up.

"What does that mean?"

"Chelsey."

She held hand up to stop me.

"We just had a great time. Can we talk about this later?"

Her doe eyes blinked, with her lips poked out in a pout.

"Fine." She jumped up and gathered her shoes and purse to leave. I rose to stop her from leaving in a huff.

"Stop acting like that." I slammed the door before she could leave, with my hands wrapped around her full figure.

"Not acting like anything."

"You forget, I've known you since you were in middle school."

"Still pisses me off the same way."

"How is that?"

"I'm tired and not in the mood to argue."

I stepped back, giving her space so she could leave, and I watched her walk out, past one of my workers and waved at them.

"What's up with Chelsey?" she asked, pointing behind his back.

"Nothing."

"Seems like she was upset."

Not up for talking about my relationship, I grabbed up the inventory list and went to check on the supplies we needed to order.

"Did you need something?" I questioned.

She rolled her eyes and flipped me off.

"I should be offended, but I'm already dealing with an angry woman."

"Then you're not surprised if I stop talking to you."

"Go back to work."

"You don't pay me enough." She stuck out her tongue and skipped off to the front desk to check someone at the counter.

⚜   2   ⚜

XAVIER

Next morning.

I carried the garbage down the walkway, opened the top, and dropped it inside, before waving over to the neighbor who constantly stuck her nose in anybody's business. Retta was in her late-sixties, widowed, and her kids lived out of the state. Since I moved to the area seven months ago, I'd gotten to know her, and she hung with my mom when she visited. Retta knew everyone's business; even Chelsey's parents came up in conversation sometimes when I was out here doing yard work or working out. I stepped back in the house, shut the screen door, and went to the kitchen to grab a glass of water, kissing the side of Chelsey's neck. She tried to move away, and I shook my head at her little attitude from last night.

"You're not talking to me today."

"Possibly."

"Peanut."

"Xavier."

"Somehow I think this has more to do with your father than me."

She dropped the spatula and turned around, glaring at me.

"My father is not the problem this time."

"What can I do to make it right?"

"We both need to compromise and spend more time together."

"I agree, but you know the second gym is taking up a lot of my time."

"And I'm happy for you but remember what matters."

"I will. So, how are things coming along at the bank?"

Chelsey shrugged and turned back around, picking up the spatula to plate the pancakes, eggs and place them on the table in front of me.

"I'm thinking of leaving the bank."

"You've always loved working there."

"I do, but my father is putting more pressure on me."

"Come work for me."

Her eyes lit up at my suggestion.

"Thank you for the offer, but that would be too much."

"Why do you say that?"

"Xavier, you ignore all the women flirting with you, but I see it, and I'd be ready to fight them."

I chuckled at her statement, and she hated the stories of how women come in the gym and want to get a one-on-one session. She even worked out in some of the class sessions. Some of the women knew she was my girlfriend, but they didn't care.

"Sorry, baby. I'll do better to put a stop to them flirting." I kissed her cheek.

"Thank you. What are your plans for today?" She scooped oatmeal in her mouth.

She wanted to go on a diet, and I often complained because in my eyes, she was perfect the way she was. I didn't care about her being a size zero or twenty. I loved every curve, stretch mark, smooth mound of her breasts, and sweet brown skin. The relationship we had was bumpy in the beginning. Her parents weren't too happy that she was dating a blue-collar type of guy with baggage from his upbringing. Plus, her family was well known in Tennessee, and my family was known as the black sheep. We made it work and became even closer, and things were looking up until recently.

"Meet up with Jordan and Mason at the gym."

"I have to see my mom, then run to the bank for a few minutes."

"Let's plan a date."

"Tonight?"

"Yeah, what do you want to do?"

Chelsey pushed her fork over into my plate and picked up a piece of pancake.

"Can we go to the club?"

"You can have whatever you want."

"What if I wanted to do something different at the club?"

"I don't share."

She snickered and stretched her hand out to palm my wrists.

"I know, but I was thinking we could try some new things out in the bedroom."

"Should have started the conversation off like that."

"Stop being so uptight." She rose, pecked me on the lips, picked her dishes up, and went to the sink.

"I told you long ago, you're mine."

I followed to put the leftover food in the trash and helped wash the dishes before showering and going off to work.

AN HOUR LATER, I WAS INSIDE MY SECOND LOCATION, teaching a class, and watched to make sure everyone was doing the steps correctly. I didn't teach as much as I used to in the beginning because the business side of things took up most of my time. I'd planned to have my assistant handle more of the workload, but I had control issues, and leaving anything up in the air would drive me crazy.

"Xavier, can you help me with my back?" LoriAnn called out from the second row. She was one of the ladies Chelsey had talked about flirting with repeatedly. rEver since she got her breast implants, she thought that would be a turn on for me, which was further from the truth. I liked my women natural, intelligent, and a great personality.

"You look to be doing okay to me," I said, standing next to her. I pushed the microphone up and turned the music volume low.

"I think I'm missing the correct pose; can you help me please?" She batted her eyelashes and smiled. I knew what she was doing, but I refused to fall into her trap, especially with Emma being here and staring. Jordan was planning on meeting me here soon, and Emma would run her mouth and say I was doing something I wasn't.

"Spread your legs a little further out. Overall, you got this," I replied, continuing to walk around the room. I checked to make sure everybody was comfortable and getting what they needed out of the session.

"All right, folks. Another great day. I hope you enjoyed it. Make sure to check the schedule for the next session."

"What if we want a private session?" LoriAnn blurted out, tossing her blond hair into a high ponytail.

"I no longer do private sessions, but my team can help you out."

"But I want you." She stepped in front of me and ran her finger down my arm.

"Xavier, have you talked to Chelsey today?"

I smirked, looking up at Emma as she stared at LoriAnn's hand on my arm.

"Yes, we're planning a date tonight. Why?"

"You have a girlfriend?" LoriAnn asked.

"He does, so I'd advise you to knock off the flirting," Emma informed her. Out of the corner of my eye, I saw Jordan hold his finger up to his lips, creeping up behind Emma.

"Excuse me—"

"LoriAnn!"

Jordan bearhugged her from behind and twirled her in a circle.

"Put me down!" she snapped, clenching her fist and hitting him on the back.

I laughed and stepped around LoriAnn to gather my bag and clean up the equipment from the class. LoriAnn took that as her cue to leave, which I was grateful for. Emma was a spit-fire like Chelsey when she was pushed.

"Man, what are you doing, messing with people." Jordan put Emma down on the floor.

"If Chelsey is not here, who else will have her back?" Emma replied.

"Not your job, Emma."

"Jordan, shut up and worry about yourself. I know you've been looking at other women," Emma fussed, took the keys out of his hands, and marched out of the room in a huff.

"Women, man." Jordan picked up one of the rugs off the floor to help me clean up.

"Is she still accusing you of stepping out?" I asked. Emma recently had a baby and worked on losing some of the baby weight, but she still felt like Jordan was cheating, even though they'd been married for a year.

"Same thing, different day. We'll be fine."

"I understand."

"My sister is acting funny."

"I think your father is starting up again."

"He was pissed about you guys living together?" Jordan asked.

"Probably, but it's mostly us not spending time together."

"You have to make it a priority. I'm taking Emma on a little couples trip."

"Where?"

I left the room, marked off the class, and blocked off the rest of my day with the front desk. Jordan went to the bar I had installed for the new location. A few minutes later, Jordan set the peach-lime smoothie on the desk, and I thanked him.

"We're heading to Jamaica for a few days."

"Who's keeping Jr.?"

"My parents."

"You guys deserve a little getaway."

"Being married comes with adjustments, so I'm not knocking Emma for feeling lonely."

My brow hiked at his admission.

"Is there something you need to tell me?"

"Bro, cut it out. I'm not cheating."

I raised my hands in shudder.

"I didn't say you were. Just need to know if I should get a spare room set for you," I joked. His eyes drew into slits.

"Not funny."

"I hear you, but what are you doing tonight?"

"Nothing but hanging with my kid and Emma."

"I'm going to the club with Chelsey."

"Spare me the details please."

"It's your fault we even know about the place."

"You always throw that in my face."

"Fuck you."

"But for real, my sister loves you. Ignore what naysayers throw your way."

"Thanks, bro." We shook hands, and I continued shuffling through orders.

"Have you thought of expanding the business more?"

"I am, and it's one cause of contention in my relationship."

"She thinks you'll have less time for her?"

"I've been on a kick of wanting everything perfect."

"That's understandable as a new businessman."

"Yeah, but I do stay here late at night sometimes, or come in extra early."

"Gotcha."

"Not good."

"Nope, especially if you want to eventually marry."

A knock at the door interrupted us, and I motioned for Mason to come in and take a seat.

"We were just talking about you."

"Whatever it is, leave me out of it please." He slugged his gym bag on the floor.

"Are you just getting in now?" I questioned.

"Yeah, I had an early meeting."

"We need a room reserved."

"Just called my assistant to hold one and tell her I said the top room."

"Thanks."

"No problem. So, how are things?" Mason picked up a piece of candy from the jar on my desk.

"Women."

"When are you planning to marry Chelsey?" he asked.

"More than likely after I have the next location up and running."

He and Jordan looked at each other.

"What?"

"All I'm going to say is that waiting too long can be disaster."

"Thanks, Oprah."

"Chelsey wants to get married," Jordan said.

"I know that, and I want to marry her, but not yet."

"Putting work before your relationship is not a good idea," Mason said.

Everyone knows I grew up poor and struggled to make ends meet once I got into what I loved to do and have the person I loved by my side. At the same time, she came from wealth and was used to having money and her lifestyle. I planned to make sure it continued once we got married.

"I got this, guys."

❦ 3 ❧

CHELSEY

I lied and told Xavier I was only visiting with my mother and then some bank work, but I failed to mention I had an appointment with my doctor because I'd felt a little off lately. I was afraid it could be something serious and not knowing would stress me out even more. Dr. Abrams wrote in her notes as I sat up from the table and pulled the gown down.

"All right, Chelsey, so how long have you been feeling off?"

"About a month now."

"Have your periods been regular?" she questioned.

"Yeah, are you saying I'm pregnant?"

"No, I will have to wait and see what the test results are."

"Extra tired from working a lot."

"Are you putting in more hours than usual?"

"Yes."

She dropped the pen, removed her glasses, and sat back in the chair.

"We talked about your workload, Chelsey."

"I know, Dr. Abrams."

"Call me Chloe, but I think it's stress."

"Really think so?"

"Not to worry. Take a vacation or cut your workload down."

"I promise I will."

"Good, I'll call you in a few days with results."

We hugged, and I got dressed and set up an appointment to come back in a few months. I picked up my phone, walked to my car, and dialed Emma's number.

"Hey, lady."

"Hello."

"Where are you? You sound windy."

"Getting in my car, leaving the store."

"Well, I'm sitting here with throw up on my boobs from your nephew."

I laughed, turned out of the parking space, and headed through the green light. I propped my phone on the stand to talk on speaker.

"Leave my baby alone."

"Your baby is messy."

"Awww, Jr. is sweet."

"That's a lie."

"You need a girls' day out. What about lunch and the spa?"

"That sounds great, but your brother has planned a trip for us."

"What! When does this happen?"

"In two weeks, Jamaica."

"That sounds exciting."

"I can't wait to be buck naked on the beach." She laughed, and I chuckled at her statement.

"Have fun for me then."

"Why don't you come with Xavier?"

"He's too busy. Plus, my schedule is mounting."

"Too much work for me."

"Change the subject. How was class earlier?"

"It was fine, besides LoriAnn's ass."

"What she do now?"

"Her usual flirting and trying to suck Xavier's dick through his shorts."

We burst into laughter at her comment. I slowed through a yellow light and made it a block away from my job.

"Girl, LoriAnn is a mess."

"She really is and so desperate."

"Let her keep on with the mess."

"Why does she think she can have my man?"

"I don't know, but you better inform her before I do."

"You're right."

"Let me call you back. This boy is crying up a storm."

"No worries. Give him a kiss for me. I just made it to work."

"Sounds good. Call me on your lunch break."

"Okay. Bye, girl."

I ended the call and shut the door, holding on my briefcase and purse. I spoke to the security guard and staff, then sauntered to my office. I dropped my bags on the floor next to my desk and hit the answering machine for messages.

"Hey, Chelsey. You have an appointment."

"Who is it? I wasn't expecting anyone."

"A Ryan Barnes," she whispered, biting her nail.

"Candice, please be professional."

"Sorry."

"Send him back here." I bent down to open my briefcase and take out the banking loans I needed to approve. I heard someone whistle, and I jumped up fast.

"Sexy."

"Huh?"

"You're sexy."

A lump formed in my throat. The dark-brown eyes staring back at me looked like a lion ready to pounce on his prey. I would never cheat, but something about this man seemed odd and familiar.

"Ryan Barnes." He stuck his hand out for a shake.

"Chelsey, president of the bank."

"I know. You don't remember, do you?"

"No, have a seat."

He chuckled, opened his jacket, and sat with his legs gaped open. Ryan looked to be as tall as Xavier with all thirty-two teeth. Dimples on both sides of his cheek, light brown skin, low trim fade.

"I worked with your father."

"Oh."

"He told me I should meet with you about my company looking to do investments."

"Well, my father was mistaken, Ryan. We're not doing investments."

"He said you'd say that."

"My father tells a lot of lies."

"I think the last time we saw each other, we had a charity event together."

"That's where I know you from."

"Yeah, a children's charity my company helped sponsor."

"I hope you find the investors, but right now, that's not something I'm interested in doing."

"No problem, thought I'd ask. What about dinner?"

I stood, and he rose out of his seat. I rounded the desk and opened the office door for him to leave.

"I have a boyfriend."

"You're still with that handyman."

"Handyman?"

He nodded.

"Xavier's a businessman with two gyms that are very well known in town and across the country."

"Ouch! Sorry, didn't mean to step on your toes."

"I know what you meant, and you can tell my father it won't work."

"Touché."

He walked out of my office, and I slammed the door behind him and started to work. I lifted the phone to put in a lunch order, and Maya poked her head in my office.

"Am I interrupting?" she asked.

"Hey! I haven't seen you in forever, Senator Hill." I reached out for a hug.

"I know. I thought I'd pop in on my way to work to say hi."

"You look gorgeous."

"So do you. How are things going around here?" She motioned around my office.

My head tilted to the side in thought, and I pursed my lips.

"Exhausting."

"I told the girls that when I'm back in town, we all should get together for a girls trip or something."

"How is everything in politics?"

"Up and down as usual."

"How precious is this little one?"

"She's beautiful, funny, and sweet. How is your family?"

"You know my brother just had a baby boy, and he's married."

"Your parents must be happy."

"They've spoiled him so much."

"Probably waiting on you to have one."

"That won't happen for a while."

"You're not interested in having a family?"

"In the future, but we're living together now, and I like it being just us."

"I get it. Mason and I were just having fun in the beginning. Soon, we just became husband and wife."

"One day I'll get there."

"Well, I won't hold you up. Get back to work." Maya reached over for a hug, and I waved goodbye. I grabbed my cell and dialed my parents at home to talk with my father.

"Hello."

"Hi, Mom."

"Hey, Chelsey."

"Is Dad there?"

"No, he's at some busy meetings."

"What happened to him retiring?" I questioned.

"Your father will never stop working."

"Well, can you relay a message that he needs to stop trying to interfere in my love life."

"What did he do?"

"You remember Ryan Barnes?"

"That name sounds familiar."

"He owns a lot of real estate properties and has a charity we contributed to."

"Oh, right, I remember."

"Yeah, he just showed up here in my office."

"Maybe he wanted to do business."

"Mom, I'm not stupid."

"All right, I'll talk with your father."

"Thanks, please tell him this was the last straw."

"Chelsey."

"I'm serious. Get over it. Xavier is my forever."

4

CHELSEY

The club was crowded tonight, and I was happy Xavier reserved a room tonight and ordered us drinks and a light meal. I removed my jewelry and stood naked in front of him as he held onto anal beads in his hand.

"Turn around," he commanded, and I nodded, doing as he instructed and climbing on top of the bed. I felt his warm hands caress my ass. I watched him pick up the bottle of lube and pop it open to prepare for what was to come.

"Take a deep breath, baby," he said. I felt an intense pressure once he pushed each bead in slowly. Clenching my teeth, I squeezed the sheets in my hand as he came up behind me and pushed my legs close together as I lay flat on my stomach. Tonight, he'd wanted to be gentle and take his time exploring my body and giving into my desires. Feeling his kisses down my back to each ass cheek, he separated and pushed his large girth in my pussy. A lump formed in my throat, knowing how good he made me come at times. Sometimes, it became a game to see if I'd squirt on command.

"Fuck me... Yes, right there," I panted, trying to push back into him. Often, he'd tell me to bring him to his knees, but he couldn't imagine what it felt like to have him moaning and rumbling under his breath.

"Shit..." He buried his nose in the pillow next to me, grinding back and forth.

"Harder, X," I cried out, needing him to lose control.

"You feel that?" he questioned, giving me punishing deep thrusts. Our skin smacked against each other until he abruptly pulled out and turned me over. He lifted me around the waist halfway, bent his legs, and slid back in to pump faster. I propped myself up with my hands, barely able to control the orgasm that lingered in my core. Something about these new tricks turned me on even more.

"Mmmm... Ohhh God... .Xavier," I screamed when he lifted me up and stepped off the bed, still holding me around the waist. I reached out to grab the back of his head and smashed my mouth on his. The tingling feeling rose, and Xavier pushed my left leg down and propped my right leg up in his arm. He thrusted from the bottom, and I felt my soul leave my body at him slamming into me hard.

"The room is spinning... Ahh!"

"Your pussy is choking my dick."

"Please can I come?" I asked.

"Damn, come now," he grunted, moved his hand, and rubbed my clit.

"Ughh... Xavier." My head fell onto his shoulder.

His tongue snaked his way through my lips. I rubbed the back of his head.

"I love it when you get flexible," he whispered in my ear.

THREE DAYS LATER.

Tonight, we had family dinner with my parents and my brother, his wife Emma. Xavier was dressed nicely, and I threw on a simple black, knee-length dress with wide straps. Xavier held my hand. and I knocked, leaning my head on his shoulder.

"Hopefully we don't stay long."

"Let's pray everybody is cool tonight." Xavier responded, knocking on the door again. The butler opened it and smiled.

"Miss Chelsey," Anderson said.

"Hi, Anderson."

I removed my coat, and he took it, hanging up, along with Xavier's. We headed into the family room and heard laughter. I smiled at my nephew in my brother's arms and glanced around the room full of guests. My mouth dropped open in shock.

"There's Chelsey," Gerald blurted out. All eyes looked at us.

Ryan was here with an older couple I assumed were his parents. He looked gorgeous with a fresh, trimmed beard. He wore a black Tom Ford suit, which I guessed from a glance because I had purchased the same thing for Xavier months back. I grew heated in annoyance that my father would stoop so low after everything we'd been through to become a family again. He promised to make an effort with me being in a relationship with Xavier, but that was all a lie from the simple fact Ryan showed up at my office. Now, he was here at their house.

"Peanut, you good."

I cleared my throat.

"Yes, I'm fine. Why do you ask?"

"You went blank for a second."

"Finally, Princess has arrived," Jordan joked, walked over to Xavier, and dapped, then gave me a hug.

"Shut up, Jordan." I pushed him in the shoulder.

"Not my fault you take forever to get dressed," Jordan complained. I rolled my eyes and grabbed my nephew.

"Come here, Auntie's baby."

Emma passed him over, and I kissed his chunky cheeks. I was planning to ignore everyone except Jordan and Emma. You would never catch me disrespecting my parents, but I was good with ignoring them to keep the peace and from keeping Xavier out of the games my father was playing. I walked down the hall to the kitchen to grab a bottle for Jr. and a drink for me.

"Are you planning to ignore me all night?"

My back stiffened. I felt my skin get warm, as my nephew continued sucking on his bottle without a care in the world. I turned around to face the culprit and put on a fake smile so the chef wouldn't freak out.

"Mr. Barnes, it's nice to see you again."

I pulled the bottle from my Jr.'s mouth and held him on my shoulder to pat his back.

"Is that your boyfriend?"

"Mr. Barnes, how is that any of your business?"

"You're cute when you're upset."

"I know. My man tells me that all the time."

He smirked and slid his tongue over his top lip.

"Chelsey, you good?" Xavier approached, stood to the side of me, and stared at Ryan.

"Ryan, and you are?" He reached a hand out toward Xavier.

"Someone you don't want to know about."

5

XAVIER

The guy looked from me toward Chelsey, like they held a secret that shouldn't get out, but I knew all her old boyfriends. If you want to call them boyfriends; we ran every guy away who tried to talk to her.

"No offense, but Chelsey was introducing me to her nephew."

"You see him. Anything else?"

"What's your name again?"

"I didn't give it."

Chelsey held her hand out, blocking me from charging at him.

"Ryan, I think you better go," she said.

The cockiness on his face went away. He seemed more nervous when my fists drew at my side. It didn't play about a lot of things, and Chelsey was one of them. I caught on as soon as we walked in that her parents were trying to set her up with him. All this time of him pretending to be cool with me was fake and phony. For Chelsey's sake, I never said a word, but tonight went overboard.

"You okay." She wrapped her arm around my waist and

leaned into my chest. I took Jr. out of her hold and held him in my arms.

"I'm fine, but your little boyfriend's going to get his ass kicked."

She slapped me on the chest.

"He's not my boyfriend."

"You sure, because he's really working on trying to be."

"I already have a boyfriend."

"What's his name?"

"Xavier."

"Good girl." I bent down, ran my tongue across her lips, pushed my tongue through, and sucked on her bottom lip.

"Eww... don't do that nasty shit in front of my son," Jordan barked, grabbing his son out of my hands.

"Shut up, Jordan. You act like you don't do worse in front of him." Chelsey pinched his arm. He stepped out of her way, as she chased him around the island in the kitchen.

"Jr., you see your auntie. Nasty, man," Jordan joked, and I chuckled and held my hand up to cover my laugh.

Chelsey's face grew into a grimace.

"Stop telling him that stuff. Babies retain the stupid shit you say."

"Chelsey, are you going to ignore your parents all night?" Jordan stopped running, passed his son back to Chelsey, and grabbed a bottle of water out of the fridge.

"Yep, so don't get on my bad side, or join my list." Chelsey strolled out of the kitchen, we followed as she played with the baby.

The dining room table was set for a large party, but it was a small gathering, so this told me her parents wanted to impress him and his parents.

"Xavier, I'm glad you could come, but Chelsey said your businesses have taken off?" Lynidas asked.

I pulled the chair out for Chelsey and sat next to her. Ryan sat across next to his parents.

"Chelsey wanted me here, so I make sure to spend as much time together as we can."

"He's even thinking of opening a third fitness center," Chelsey replied.

"Does that really bring in any money?" Gerald asked.

"Daddy, we talked about this."

"Tonight is about family, and new business. Mr. Barnes is looking to expand his business." Lynidas held her glass up for toast.

"I went by Chelsey's office earlier today, but she declined my offer," Ryan said.

I clenched the napkin in my hand, as he stared at Chelsey and smirked. Swiftly I glanced at her to meet her eyes, and she quickly handed Jr. to Emma.

"Xavier, let's go." Chelsey jumped up out of her seat.

"We haven't had dinner yet, Chelsey," Lynidas said.

"I lost my appetite," Chelsey replied and walked out of the dining room.

"Ryan, I apologize for my daughter's behavior. I will get you with the right people," Gerald answered.

I saved and worked to get everything I had now and to be with Chelsey I knew she was a prize. She was expected to date a guy on a certain financial level to provide for her. For him to stand in my face after we talked and made some type of resolution. Chelsey had no problems out of our relationship.

"Let's go."

"I'll call you tomorrow, Peanut," Jordan said. She kissed her nephew on the lips, and I grasped her hand and walked out together, not looking back.

THE FOLLOWING DAY, I HAD MORRIS AND WARREN FOLLOW up on Ryan Barnes and his business. Their work not only involved securing events but delved into background checks and private investigation if needed. I knocked on the door of Morris' office and waited to be let inside.

"It's open!" he called out.

I turned the knob and walked in to see Lisa sitting on the edge of his desk.

"Hey, Xavier!" Lisa said.

"How are you, Lisa?"

We hugged, and I sat in the chair across from his desk.

"I'm doing good. Actually, I'm meeting Chelsey later for shopping and lunch."

y"Try not to spend too much of my money," Morris blurted out. She rolled her eyes, pecked him on the lips, and grabbed her purse to leave. Morris opened the desk drawer, pulled a yellow envelope, and tossed it on top of the desk in front of me.

"What did you find?"

I flipped it over and took out stacks of photos and documents with Ryan's name on the label.

"He's looking to make a name for himself, working with a lot of big-time people."

"Looks like he's skimmed some money off the top."

"He's good, but most importantly, Chelsey was right to not work with him."

"Did you tell her?"

He shook his head.

"No, I thought it should come from you."

"Yeah, her father is adamant about doing business with him." I looked at the numbers and noticed a lot of money changing hands.

"You'll see even more photos of Chelsey there at the club and work."

My nose flared looking over the photos he had taken of my

girl and me together. This was a game to him, and I wasn't one to play games when it came to my woman.

"What do you want to do?"

Irritation at him grew, and my pulse raced.

"I'll handle him."

I stood, and Morris jumped up and held his hand out to block me from leaving.

"I didn't give you that information to possibly end up in jail."

"Don't worry. I'll have a little conversation with him and be on my way."

Morris chucked his chin up.

"Just a conversation."

"I'm a businessman first."

"Yeah, but we both know how you are about Chelsey."

I growled at his comment, bringing up the past when Mason mistook her for someone else, and we almost got into a fight.

"Sounds like you're worried about me."

"Any friend of Lisa's, I have to protect. Chelsey is her friend, which means we look out for each other."

"Thanks, Morris, but I promise not to kill him. A black eye, now that's different."

I smacked the papers against my hand and marched out of his office to find Mr. Barnes and catch up on some things.

❧ 6 ☙

CHELSEY

The mall was crowded, and I held two bags in my hands from Lane Bryant. I needed some more comfortable clothing before the winter time got here and some rain boots I'd been eyeing for the longest time. My father tried calling me earlier today, and I ignored his call and met up with the girls for a day of pampering before Emma went on her trip.

"Let's go in here." Emma pointed at Victoria's Secret. We followed, and I saw a black silk robe with a matching bra set. I picked it up to check the price and look for my size.

"You ready for your trip, Emma?" Lisa asked.

"Yes, I can't wait to be on a beach with my boo." Emma picked through the row of red stockings and bras.

"How long are you guys going for?"

"A week," Emma replied, holding a bra up to show us.

"That's cute. Try a pink or lavender color," I suggested, going to the rack of tights and pajama pants.

"Why didn't we get invited?" Lisa wondered.

"For real, I'm done filming for two months. I need a vacation," Kyla pouted, holding three pairs of socks and thongs.

"This is a reconnection trip for me and Jordan," Emma answered, and I nodded in agreement. She'd been working nonstop as a stay-at-home mom. Plus, with Jordan working nonstop, they needed time together as much as me and Xavier.

"Well, we can plan something for couples next time."

"I vote for that." Maya joined us, and we all screamed and crowded around her as security stood, blocking people off. I should have asked to have the store closed for us to shop privately since we had a politician and actress, along with Lisa in attendance.

"Maybe we should get out of here. The place is getting a lot of attention," Emma suggested.

"Are you done shopping?" I questioned.

"Just need these." She held up a thong set, switched over to the register, and I laughed.

"You won't even have that on long enough once Jordan sees you wearing them."

"That's true. Our love life has been in a little rut," Emma complained.

"Preaching to the choir." I raised my hand.

"Strong women with hot guys, and no time to fuck. What is the world coming to now?" Lisa joked, and I chortled and placed money down to pay on my nightgown set.

"I could go for something to eat."

"Where do we want to go?" Lisa asked.

"Try that pizza place on Third and Poplar Avenue," Kyla said.

"No, I'm tired of crowds. Let's go to my place and order food," I said.

All the girls agreed and finished paying for their items. Lisa and Kyla piled into my car, and Maya told the security team to follow her in mine since Emma drove her car, and she would ride with her.

Thirty minutes later, we sat out by the pool in the back with bottles of wine, fruit, cheese tray, with a variety of meals from salads, fish tacos, and pizza. I opened a bottle of wine and served the drinks, while Maya fixed the plates as they lounged near the cabana deck.

"So, Morris wants me to move to Vegas," Lisa blurted out, taking a gulp of her wine.

All of them gasped in response, and I sipped my drink.

"What do you want?" Maya asked.

"I might feel the same way." Lisa shrugged her shoulders.

"Warren and I are splitting time between Vegas and here. He's also expanding into Chicago," Kyla told me.

"I feel like Xavier and I are drifting apart."

"Wait! Why am I the last to know all this?" Maya argued.

"You're a senator, wife, and mother, Maya."

"We can't come to you with all our problems." Lisa walked up to the table and poured more wine.

"I understand, but I feel like our little group is growing apart. I just met Emma." Maya pointed toward Emma and bit into her pizza.

"We have to make a promise to stay in touch."

"No matter what, we'll always have our group chats." Lisa laughed and shimmied in her seat.

"This is like a full-circle moment."

"What do you mean?" Emma said.

"Because of you, we went to Club Seek, and they found men." I pointed at Emma.

"Ohhh, that's right. That's for helping me find the best pussy eater in the world." Lisa snapped her finger and held her glass up in the air. Everyone burst into laughter as Emma spat out her drink.

"Lisa, some things you can keep to yourself," Maya fussed.

"I know, Maya, but don't act like Mason doesn't have your toes circling," Lisa replied.

"I've been feeling a little off lately," I said, quickly draining my glass of alcohol. I reached for another bottle, and Lisa slapped my hand away.

"What do you mean off?"

"Tired, not able to eat. I went to the doctor."

"When did this happen?"

"A few days ago."

"When were you going to tell us?"

"Dr. Abrams is running tests."

"Call her." Lisa dug into her purse and pulled her cell phone out.

"Her office is probably closed. It's going on four in the afternoon." I looked down at my watch.

"We're best friends, almost sisters. Hell, she's your sister-in-law, and you kept this from her," Lisa argued.

"Maybe you're pregnant," Kyla blurted, grabbed some tacos off the table.

"I'm not ready for that."

"You're never ready," Maya and Emma said at the same time.

"What did Xavier say?" Lisa questioned.

"He doesn't know."

"Chelsey," Emma fussed.

"Our schedules are crazy right now, then there was the mess with my father at the house."

"What happened to that?" Lisa questioned.

Emma and I peered at each other.

"My dad tried to set me up."

"With another guy? Like a date?" Lisa asked.

"More like a marriage," Emma muttered.

"Had the guy come to my job, then my parents' house with his parents," I said.

"Wow," Maya said.

"I refuse to call them."

"Even your mom." Kyla passed Emma some of her food and sat at the edge of the chair.

"I'll call her in a few days, but it's mostly my dad."

"You're doing the right thing. Ignore him," Lisa said.

"Xavier was ready to kick his ass at the table." I chuckled.

"That plays no games about you," Kyla said.

"I know."

❦ 7 ❧

XAVIER

I *pushed him up against the wall, held my arm up against his neck, and placed pressure with my fists balled up.*

My thoughts went from talking to wanting to punch, then shoot him in my mind. I didn't need to be away from Chelsey, so I optioned for talking unless he got out of hand.e

"Mr. Barnes, Xavier is here to see you."

"Send him in, Rachel."

She waved me in, and I smiled politely and watched her close the door. I locked it and held the envelope in my hand. He stood, buttoning his jacket behind his desk.

"Xavier, what do I owe for this visit?" Ryan picked up the envelope I had tossed on his desk.

"You've been stalking my girl."

He chuckled.

"I don't need to stalk."

"Oh, because you have money, right?"

"Money, charm, world class."

"Look, you piece of shit!"

"I can have security here in a split second."

"Fuck your security."

"It's not my fault her parents want her with me."

"Chelsey doesn't want you."

"Did she say that?"

"I'm going to say this for the last time, because I know she already spoke to you. Leave Chelsey alone."

"Or what?"

"Find out."

"If we do business together, maybe I'll back off."

I chortled at his comment.

"The business you're stealing from me, right?"

"You can't prove that."

"Try me and see. If you come in contact with Chelsey or her father."

He blew out a breath and waved me off. I started to charge toward him.

"Okay, I'll stay away." He held his arms up in surrender.

"That's a safe bet."

❦

I DOUBLE CHECKED THE COLLAR AROUND HER NECK AND peered in her eyes as she watched my every move. Tonight, we decided to take it another step further with her chained by a spreader bar separating her legs and hands in suspension in the air. Her curvy full figure was a beautiful sight to see, and I decided to turn the video on. I needed a reminder of this for when we were alone again and needed inspiration. Chelsey moaned as my hand ran down from her ankle to her inner thigh. I smelled her sweet arousal, and my dick hardened and jumped, ready to dig into her walls.

"She's already screaming for me."

Chelsey nodded and gasped when I slid not one, but two fingers inside.

"Taste yourself, baby." I lifted my finger to her lips.

"Mmmm..."

"You're about to be fucked so hard."

"Please."

"You're my queen, remember that."

"You're my king."

I couldn't wait any longer and pushed forward to her asshole. I felt her tense up and lovingly tweaked her nipples, kissed her lips, and teased her clit to loosen her up.

"Just a little more, baby."

"Oh... Yes." She gasped.

"Oh, fuck!" I moaned and felt her rock back and forth, meeting my thrusts.

"Xavier!"

"I need you to come on my tongue." I suddenly pulled out, dropped to my knees, sucking, slurping, and twirling my tongue on her wet, gushy sex. Hearing her screams and shouts of pleasure gave me motivation to never lose sight of what I had in front of me. My past could never compare to what my future looked like before me.

"Shittt..." she moaned and squirted in my mouth, and I stood back up, shoved my dick in her tight pussy, and muttered more curse words under my breath once I came behind her. I bent over, deepened our kiss, and sucked on her tongue. Seeing the exhaustion on her face, I stood and reached for the towel from the back of the chair, wiped us off, and unhook the chains.

"You ready for bed?"

"I'm ready to go home."

"As you wish..."

I kissed the top of her forehead and helped her down, and we redressed and left for home.

THE NEXT DAY, I DROVE WITH CHELSEY TO HER DOCTOR'S follow-up appointment to get her results. I was more nervous than she was, and I couldn't fathom her being sick and not waking up to her face every day.

"Stop worrying." I held her hand up, kissing her palm.

"Trying to stay positive, but what if..."

"No what ifs. We don't think like that."

"Thank you for coming with me."

"Never worry about me being at your side."

"So, something interesting happened early today when you were in the shower," Chelsey said.

"What?"

"My father called and apologized."

"Your father?" I turned at the light into the parking structure, went to a spot near the door, and cut the car off.

"Yes, I know."

"What did he say?"

"He loves me and said Ryan's not going to bother me again."

"I'm happy to hear that, baby."

"Xavier."

"Yeah?" I opened the passenger door to help her out.

"Did you do something to Ryan?"

"Chelsey, you know me, baby."

"That's the point."

"Stop worrying about somebody that isn't in her world view." I lifted her chin, pressed a kiss on her lips, and smacked her on the ass. Holding the door open, she swished in front of me, making me adjust myself.

"Hi Chelsey, the doctor is ready for you."

"Great, thank you."

"Follow me back." The office assistant pushed the door open and let us in to have a seat to wait.

"Are you nervous?" Chelsey questioned.

I reached over and grasped both her hands. She looked into my eyes.

"No reason to be nervous. We're good, and you'll be fine." I bent down, slid my tongue over her upper lip, and wrapped her hands around me.

With a knock at the door, the doctor stepped in and cleared her throat.

"Dr. Abrams." Chelsey giggled and wiped her lipstick off my lips.

"Xavier, good to see you again," she said.

"You too, Doc."

"Tell me the truth," Chelsey asked.

"I ran every test, and you're fine. You need to relax and take a vacation," the doctor replied.

"Seriously?" Chelsey said.

"No issues at all?"

"None. She's just stressed and needs to calm down. Her blood pressure is a little high," the doctor answered, pulling out her records.

"Thank you, Doctor."

"No problem. I like you, Chelsey, and want you to stay focused," the doctor said.

"I promise... self-care going forward," Chelsey promised.

❧ 8 ❧

CHELSEY

A month later.

I groaned, slamming the alarm off, and rolled over to feel Xavier's side of the bed was empty. I opened one eye and looked around the room. Then Xavier, wearing a pair of boxer briefs, sauntered back into the bedroom from the fog coming from the bathroom.

"Get up, sleepyhead."

"Why! This is supposed to be a vacation," I whined, falling back under the covers.

"As soon as you get up, we can have one." Xavier climbed on the bed and tickled me under the cover.

"Stop!" I screamed, trying to crawl away from him.

"Not until you get up."

"Fine, I'm up."

"Great, per doctor's orders, I want you to relax." Xavier jumped out of bed and extended a hand for me to take.

"What's the plan for today?"

"You shower, have breakfast, and then we head to the beach."

"It's gorgeous here."

"Jordan was able to get a great discount on a last-minute flight for us, so I wanted to fly you out and enjoy this weekend together."

"You didn't have to do that." I turned the shower on and stripped out of the pajamas I had picked up at Victoria's secret.

"I know, but I wanted to enjoy it all to myself."

"Well, Jamaica is the place to be."

"Might end up wanting to buy a place out here."

"Couldn't hurt to look around." I closed the shower door, grabbing the resort body wash and towel.

"Maybe not today, but we will."

"How about you come and join me?" I pushed the door back open for him to get a glimpse of me in soap suds.

"As tempting as you look, I need to get dressed and make sure breakfast is ready."

"Ugh... you're no fun," I shouted from the other side of the door.

"Later. I'll make it up to you."

❦

Two hours after getting dressed and eating breakfast, we went out to the local shops and walked around, meeting new people and sightseeing. I wanted to go to the beach later, once the sun set, and possibly get a quickie in before we went to bed. Xavier didn't mind, but the shopping part annoyed him because of the amount of stuff I bought. We had to grab a car service to send it all back to the resort and come back to do a second round of shopping.

"This drink is amazing, babe."

"Don't drink too much. I need you ready and aware for tonight."

"Oh, I'll be ready."

"Listen, have you spoken to your father before we came on the trip?"

"Why do you have to spoil the day?"

"I'm not trying to spoil our day."

"Then leave my father out of the conversation."

"Chelsey, at some point you'll need to speak with him."

"I'll talk to my mom."

"Great, but don't isolate your father out."

"Why not?"

"One day, you may need him."

"I have my brother."

"Glad to hear, but a girl needs her father."

He was right. I stayed in touch with my mom cover the past few weeks after the dinner incident. Jordan said he argued back and forth with my dad on my behalf, and I thanked him for stepping in because that man always thought he was right.

I put the drink down on the table, stared out to the ocean, and decided to be spontaneous for once and run out to the beach and let loose.

"Chelsey! Chelsey!" Xavier shouted, ran behind me, and picked me up.

"Ahhh!"

"Woman, what are you doing?"

"I want to get in the water. Put me down."

"Don't scare me like that."

He put me on the ground. I looked to my left, then right, and smirked. I wiggled my brows, lifted my dress, and tossed it on the ground.

"Come catch me," I purred and ran off toward the ocean.

I splashed in, feeling the cool waters. Xavier's eyes darkened,, and I knew the beat was coming out. He'd make me pay for this little rendezvous.

"You're going to pay for that."

"You have to catch me first."

I swam out a little farther, away from any crowds, and he caught up to me, wrapped his arms around my waist, and pulled me into a kiss.

"Mmmmm...." he moaned, sucked on my lips, and gripped my breasts.

I threw my head back as he peppered kisses along my neck and shoulder. I locked my legs around his waist and felt him push in, stroking me slowly.

"Ughh... Xavier," I panted, tightening my grip to help balance my weight.

"Shit... We need to take this inside."

"Okay... Ahh."

Xavier pulled out of me, swam back to the beach, and led me back to the resort. We went to the shower and ended up back in bed, finishing what I started earlier. Later that evening, after going three rounds, I set up a nice dinner with all his favorites and placed everything on the deck. We sat under the stars and moon, eating and talking.

"You ever think about getting married and having kids?"

"Where did that come from?"

I cut into my calamari and took a piece.

"We never talked about the future."

"You're my future. Wherever you are, I'm there."

"I get that, but you have a booming business. It takes you away."

"Our business."

"Xavier."

"Chelsey, you know my past. It's not pretty."

"Let's drop it."

XAVIER

I'd been holding onto the news that my fitness center would be opening another location and the guys investing to expand it even further. They thought it would be great to open a division in New York, and I was planning to scout some locations. Telling Chelsey now would only start an argument, after bringing up the topic of kids.

"Listen."

"No, I don't want to fight. This is about us enjoying ourselves."

"We are, but I hate to see you pout, so we can shelve this conversation."

"Sure."

"What do you want to do tomorrow?"

"Maybe go scuba diving."

"We can try that."

"Something that gets us really engulfed in the scenery."

"Whatever you want, sweetheart."

"Are you full?"

"I'm stuffed. This was good," I said.

"It's getting late. You want to watch a movic?"

"Yeah, it'll probably put me to sleep."

We grabbed the bottle of wine and stepped in the living room to set up a movie. She grabbed a blanket out of the bedroom, and I poured us another glass of wine and placed her feet in my lap.

"I could get used to this."

"What, being spoiled?"

"You love spoiling me." She poked her lips out for a kiss, I leaned over, pecked her lips, then rubbed a hand up and down her thigh.

"I do."

"Good."

Two hours later, we were startled out of a sound sleep at the ringing of a cell phone. I looked around and noticed it was her phone ringing.

"Babe, your phone is ringing." I nudged her in the shoulder.

"Huh."

"Your brother is calling."

"Oh... hello," she answered groggily.

She sat up quickly, with a perplexed expression.

"Is he all right!" she shouted.

"What's wrong?"

"Okay, we're leaving now." She hung up the phone and jumped off the couch.

"Chelsey, what's going on."

"We have to go back home; Dad is in the hospital."

I stopped her from pacing and pulled her in my arms to help calm her down. She started to hyperventilate.

"He's going to be fine; I need you to breathe for me, baby."

"Xavier, I can't lose my dad."

"You won't, I promise."

"We need to get a flight out."

"Just pack your things, and I'll handle everything else." I

kissed her on the forehead, grabbed our phones, and made some calls to get us back to town fast.

❧

I STOOD OFF TO THE SIDE AS CHELSEY LAID HER HEAD ON HER father's chest, while the monitors beeped. The look of relief on her face and his when we made it through those doors must have helped his recovery. He had a mild heart attack and needed to relax, cut out any stress for a while. Jordan stayed up here until we arrived and then went home to be with Emma and his son. Her mom was sleeping in the corner. Chelsey continued talking with her father, and some type of resolution was had because smiles crossed her face and his. Probably knocking on death's door helped him to see that he needed to change his ways and rethink trying to control his kids' lives.

"We'll be up here tomorrow, Daddy," Chelsey said and kissed him on the cheek. He nodded, letting her hand go.

"Xavier," he said.

"Yes, sir." I kicked my foot off the wall, treading toward the end of the bed.

"I'm sorry for everything."

"Me too."

"You're like a son to me, and I treated you horrible."

"No stress, Daddy," Chelsey said.

"Stop smothering me, Chelsey."

He waved her off, and Chelsey rolled her eyes.

He's for sure back to normal," Chelsey muttered.

I chuckled and clasped her hand, leading her out of the hospital room to head home for the night. The next morning, Jordan called to drop off Jr. with Chelsey to keep him while he and Emma helped their mom bring their father home. Standing in the kitchen, I poured coffee and set the table for breakfast, watching her stroll with him in her arms.

"He looks like your brother more and more."

I motioned for her to sit down.

"I know, it's scary."

"How's your dad doing?"

"Better. He has to change his diet and cut out stress."

"Something you know well about."

"I'm going to spend more time with you and my nephew." She lifted him in her arms, and he giggled.

"You look good with a baby in your arms."

She smirked and passed him over to me.

"He's a big boy." Chelsey kissed me on the lips, took her seat again, and poured syrup on her waffles.

"I'm still processing my brother having a kid and Dad almost dying."

"It's going to take time."

"Glad to spend that time with you."

"We already went for two rounds before he got here. Control yourself, Peanut."

"Ughh, I hate when you call me that."

"I know."

"Not the same little kid who had a crush on you when I was younger."

I placed the bottle in Jr.'s mouth and watched him stare into my eyes. I smiled at the innocence across his face.

"You mean the same one who approached me and said they wanted to F.U.C.K."

Her head fell back in laughter.

"He's a baby; he doesn't understand a word you said."

"Doesn't matter. I want to do what my parents didn't do."

"Which is?"

"Protected."

"You're going to be a great dad one day."

"Long as I have you."

EPILOGUE

One year later.

I closed my eyes and pictured myself on a beach with all my family and friends, laughing and dancing together. The relationship I built with Xavier was a long time coming, and we weathered the storm.

"Chelsey! Push one more time," the doctor demanded. The sweat on my forehead and brow dripped down my nose and cheeks. I did the breathing exercises to keep steady and pushed one more time. I felt a lightness in my body when I heard the cries of my son.

"Chelsey, he's beautiful," Mom said.

I was in a daze and barely could keep my eyes open from the ten hours of labor to get our child here safely. Xavier held him in his arms and walked back over to me, placing him on my bare chest to do skin to skin.

"He looks just like you," I cooed and rubbed the back of his head. Xavier bent down and kissed me on the lips.

"Thank you, Peanut."

"Thank you for being an amazing friend, lover, and husband."

"I can't believe I wasted so long to make you mine."

"It was meant to be like this."

"You're right. Get some rest though; I'll stay up with him."

"What do you want to name him?"

"Michael Xavier."

"He's perfect like his mommy."

He yawned and opened his eyes briefly, and I teared up again, seeing the same ocean-blue eyes like his father. My son would be a heartrbreaker, and I needed to prepare myself to not hold on too tight.

"He's starting to cry; I think he's hungry."

"I'll feed him, then you can rock him to sleep," I told Xavier, who helped me pull the gown down and get Michael to latch on properly to right breast. It hurt a little, but I knew this was what I wanted in the beginning when the doctor said I was too stressed and needed to relax. I took her advice and cut my hours at work and spent more time with Xavier, going on trips together. One of those trips ended up being the night we conceived Michael. Now I had all the blessings and the man of my dreams, who I had loved since I could remember.

⚜

Two years later.

"Do you Xavier take Chelsey to be your husband, in sickness and in health?"

When I thought of my life after giving birth to my son, I never took that day for granted, even when I married Xavier. Here we were years later, and I stopped working at the bank. He opened up a chain of fitness centers, and I was a stay-at-home mom with Michael our little Angel. Xavier wanted more kids, we talked about waiting until Michael is older, in school. After we had our first, I couldn't deny seeing the joy from my family growing.

"I do." Xavier smiled and held onto my hands. We stood in the backyard of our home he had built. Xavier became a multimillionaire, and no one would ever know. We lived just as modest as we did before.

"Do you, Chelsey—"

"I do!" I yelled excitedly, and our friends and family laughed. The yard was decorated in white and pink with rose petals on the ground. A large sign with our names and the kids hung over the balcony.

"I now pronounce you husband and wife."

Xavier didn't even wait for him to finish, smashing his lips onto my mouth and palming my butt. I extended my arms around his neck. Xavier surprised me with renewing our vows, and I had a surprise for him later when we went to our own private club in the basement.

I HOPE YOU ENJOYED CHELSEY AND XAVIER'S STORY. PLEASE also check out the bonus scene next.

If you love brother's best friend romance then you'll love **"Sensual" here** https://books2read.com/u/49lYYM with a host of characters intertwined.

Check out BodyguardRomance here ***"Protecting Bria"*** https://books2read.com/u/bQJkjd

Please also check out my ***"Haven"*** https://books2read.com/u/4jAvyZ a steamy enemies to lovers romance.

Have you checked out **"His Peace Her Pleasure"** click here https://books2read.com/u/3JJroP a billionaire, steamy romance.

❧ 10 ❧

BONUS SCENE: XAVIER

Our relationship started here, so I wanted to celebrate at the place we frequented together and spark up what made us take the step to be together. The kids were home with her parents for the day, so I blocked off the day to spend time with her on our anniversary. She wore a sexy crossbody Ivy Park workout fit. All her curves and fat ass poked out that I loved to taste at night when we were alone.

"Xavier!" she gasped when my hand went to her lower back and peeled back the shorts. She kicked them off, showing only a red thong. I smacked her ass, watched it jiggle, and kissed each cheek.

"I want you to do five pushups."

"What do I get in return?" she questioned.

"I want you face down, ass up with me over you as you rise."

"Somehow I think this won't be an actual workout."

"It can be."

The smirk I held showed I was planning something else behind my little suggestion. I had the whole place locked down for the day and put on some music, brought drinks and food in case we needed them. She turned around, got in position, and started to drop to the floor, I pushed her legs together in the proper form. Then I removed my shirt and shorts.

"What are you doing?" She licked her lips.

"We're going to start with me behind you as you come up.:

"Your dick is going to be poking me."

"That's the point, my love."

"Somehow I knew you'd make these torturous."

"If you do a full push up, I'll give you a reward either with my tongue or my dick."

"If I can't?"

"You don't get either."

"That's not fair."

"I promise, by the end of this workout, you won't be sweaty from just pushups."

She rolled her eyes, turned around back into her normal form, and lifted, causing her ass to graze the tip of my dick.

"Oh, God."

"It's only me here, baby."

WHAT'S NEXT

WANT TO KNOW WHAT HAPPENS next?

Follow me on Bookbub and social media today.

Reviews are the lifeblood of the publishing world. They're read, appreciated, and needed. Please consider taking the time to leave a few words on wherever you buy books. Sign up for updates and sneak peeks at the site below.

304 PUBLISHING COMPANY

WE SHOWCASE AUTHORS writing African American, Interracial, Women's Fiction, Urban Romance, Erotic, and Contemporary Romance novels. Along with Thriller, Suspense, Poetry, Beauty, and Style Books. Thank you for taking the time out to visit. Join our mailing list to stay updated with new releases and blog posts.

Catalogue of Releases by Keke Renée:
- •Wet Heat (Wet Heat Series Book 1)
- •Every Time We Touch Novelette (Wet Heat Book 2 Series)
- •His Peace, Her Pleasure
- •Baby, It's Cold Outside
- •Love Don't Live Here Anymore, Vanessa Andrew Book 1
- •Love Don't Live Here Anymore, Isabella Andrew Book 2
- •One Night Only-A Novelette (Love by Design Book 1)
- •Cassian and Savannah (Love by Design Book 2)
- •Deidra's Love (Love by Design Book 3)
- •Protecting Bria (Special Force Operation Alphas)

Thank you so much for reading.

If you enjoyed the crazy ride and decide to leave a review, we'd appreciate the support.

DEDICATION

I WANT TO THANK FIRST readers for loving these characters so much and waited so love for them to come back.

ACKNOWLEDGMENTS

I CAN'T MENTION ENOUGH the support and dedication of my author buddies for keeping me uplifted. My behind-the-scenes team of beta readers, editors, designers, and more. As a writer, I continue to strive for the best, and I appreciate everyone who reads my work. Without your continual feedback, I wouldn't be on this path, letting doubts slip away.

ABOUT THE AUTHOR

A Tennessee native and CA dreaming Author Keke Renee is living and striving to continue her passion of writing Short Story romances from Erotic, Women's Fiction, Romantic Suspense, Paranormal and Urban fiction.